The Old Woman and the Eagle

by

Idries Shah

HOOPOE BOOKS

nce upon a time,
when cups were plates
and when knives and forks grew in
the ground, there was an old woman
who had never seen an eagle.

One day, an eagle was flying high in the sky and decided to stop for a rest. He swooped down and landed — where do you think?

He landed right at
the front door of the
old woman's house.

The old woman took a long, hard look at the eagle and said, "Oh my, what a funny pigeon you are!"

She figured he was a pigeon, you see, because although she had never seen an eagle, she had seen lots of pigeons.

"I am not a pigeon at all,"
said the eagle, drawing
himself up to his full height.

"Nonsense!" said the old woman. "I've lived for more years than you've got feathers in your wings, and I know a pigeon when I see one."

"If you're so sure that I'm a pigeon," said the eagle, "then why do you say I'm a funny pigeon?"

"Well, just look at your beak," said the old woman. "It's all bent. Pigeons have nice, straight beaks.

And look at those claws of yours! Pigeons don't have long claws like that.

And look at the feathers on top of your head! They are all messed up and need to be brushed down. Pigeons have nice, smooth feathers on their heads."

And before the eagle could reply, she got hold of him and carried him into the house.

She took her clippers and trimmed his claws until they were quite short.

She pulled on his beak
until it was quite straight.

And she brushed down
the lovely tuft of feathers
on top of his head until
it was quite flat.

"Now you look more like a pigeon!" said the old woman. "That's so much better!"

But the eagle didn't feel any better. In fact, he felt quite sad.

As soon as the old woman let him go he flew to the top of a tree. As he was sitting there wondering what to do, another eagle came along and alighted on the bough beside him.

"Well, well," said the new bird. "Aren't you a funny looking eagle!"

"Well, at least you know I'm an eagle," said the first eagle. "Thank goodness for that!"

"What happened to you?" asked the new eagle.

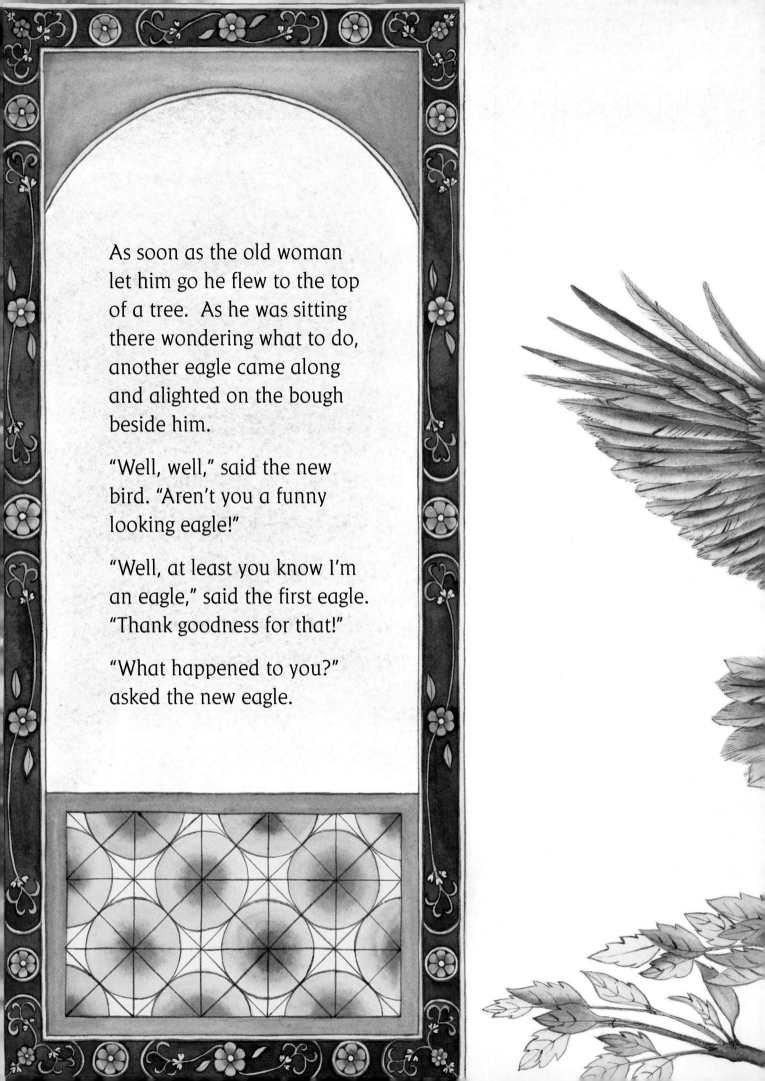

"Well," said the first eagle, "An old woman thought I was a pigeon.

And since pigeons don't have long claws, she trimmed my claws.

And since pigeons don't have hooked beaks, she straightened my beak.

And since pigeons don't have tufts of feathers on their heads, she brushed my tuft down."

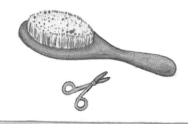

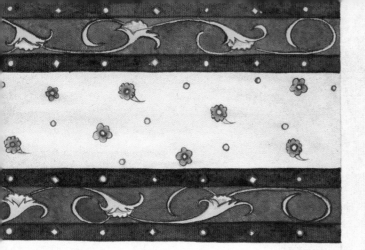

"She must be a very foolish old woman, indeed," said the new eagle.

And with that, he took a brush from under his wing, and he brushed the first eagle's feathers back into a tuft.

And with his claws he bent the eagle's beak down until it was nicely rounded once again.

"There now!" he said, "you look like an eagle again. Don't worry about your claws, they'll soon grow back."

"Thank you, my friend!" said the first eagle.

"Think nothing of it," said his new friend.

"But remember this," he continued, "there are a lot of silly people in the world who think that pigeons are eagles, or that eagles are pigeons, or that all sorts of things are other things.

And when they are silly like that, they do very foolish things. We must be sure to keep away from that silly old woman and the people like her."

And with that, the eagles flew back to their own country and returned to their own nests.

And they never went near that silly old woman again.

And so everyone lived happily ever after.